T0199137

Destiny's Day at the Zoo

J.T. Carruthers

ISBN: Softcover   978-1-9845-4800-9
        Hardcover   978-1-9845-4801-6
        EBook   978-1-9845-4799-6

Print information available on the last page

Rev. date: 08/17/2018

To order additional copies of this book, contact:
Xlibris
1-888-795-4274
www.Xlibris.com
Orders@Xlibris.com

Destiny's Day at the Zoo

Hello! My name is Destiny. I'm so excited because today is Bring Your Child to Work Day! I get to spend the day with my dad at the zoo. It's going to be so much fun as I learn about the animals while helping to feed and care for them. I love animals, like my dad, and when I grow up I want to follow in his footsteps and work at a zoo. So come follow me as we begin our day!

"So, Daddy, what's the first thing we are going to do when we get to the zoo?" I asked.

"We have to prepare the animals' food," he replied.

"Can I help?" I asked.

"Of course!" he said.

"Yay!"

"Today, the elephants are due for their baths," Dad said.

"Oh, boy!"

"You can help me with the baby calf too," Dad said.

"A baby! Oh, boy! I'm so excited!"

Dad smiled.

"Now, Destiny, as we go about our day, please let me know if you feel tired so we can go to one of the many beautiful shaded areas to relax and watch the animals."

"I'd like that."

My dad told me that I was going to meet many wonderful people who work at the zoo and that I would see how everyone works together as a team.

"I may also have a few surprises for you," Dad said with a smile.

"Oh, please tell me!" I pleaded.

"You will just have to wait," he said with a chuckle.

"Okay," I sighed.

"Are you ready for an adventurous day?" Dad asked.

"I sure am!" I replied.

"Be ready with your camera. You never know what you will see!"

"Don't worry, Daddy. I'm ready!"

We walked through the main entrance of the zoo and headed for the kitchen. We set out all kinds of fruit, vegetables, meats, nuts, and grains to feed the animals, and we put the food in various containers and trays to place into the zoo's truck. We also had rakes and shovels to clean the enclosures, as well as some fresh hay. My dad explained how each zookeeper has a list of animals to care for daily.

"The first stop, zebras!" Dad said as he closed the truck door.

"I love zebras!" I said excitedly.

We laid out the hay, alfalfa pellets, and fruit for the zebras. My dad told me that they spend most of their time eating. "I like the sound of that," I chuckled. We watched the zebras roam about the large enclosure. They're such amazing animals, I thought as I took several pictures of them.

"Zebras," Dad said, "are very social animals and live in herds in the deserts and grasslands."

"Are their stripes all alike?" I asked.

"No, there are no two zebra stripe patterns alike. Their stripes act as a type of camouflage to protect them against predators, and their stripe patterns are as distinctive as our fingerprints are to us."

"Tell me something else about zebras, Dad," I asked.

"Okay. Do you see the striped wall with black and white zebra patterns? Well, zebras are attracted to black and white stripes, so they will go over to the wall and stand by it."

"I think they're pretty cool," I said. "So, if I wore black and white clothes, would it stand next to me?" I asked.

"Your human scent would prevent that, but an interesting idea."

When we finished caring for the zebras, we moved on to the giraffes. Giraffes are so beautiful and extremely tall. My dad said that giraffes are the tallest mammals in the world and grow on average around fourteen to nineteen feet tall. It's amazing! You don't realize just how big and beautiful these animals are until you get up close to them. I saw two young calves roaming about, but not far from their mothers.

"Oh, my goodness, they are so adorable!" I said.

My dad and I prepared several pounds of leaves, flowers, seedpods, and fruits for the giraffes and climbed up some steps to fill their containers. One giraffe came over to me, and I got to feed him some fruit. It was way cool! I laughed when I saw how long its tongue was. He tickled my hand when he grabbed the food.

"Dad, how long are their tongues?" I asked, still giggling.

"Giraffes have very long tongues, Destiny. They measure about twenty-one inches long." He also told me that giraffes can eat up to 145 pounds of food in one day, and, just like zebras, giraffes do not share the same patterns. Each one has a distinctive spotted coat.

"That was fun, feeding the giraffe," I said with a smile.

"I'm glad you had fun. I know that I always enjoy feeding my friends," Dad said happily.

"Now, Destiny, do you want to have a rest, or would you like to go see the flamingos?"

"I want to see the flamingos!" I said.

We climbed back into the truck and drove to the flamingos. We had some small fish, anchovies, shrimp, and crabs in containers placed on the floor of the front seat.

Boy, was it stinky!

"Destiny, did you know that eating shrimp causes the beautiful shade of pink in the flamingos?" Dad asked.

"No, I didn't. If I eat shrimp, would I turn pink?" I asked.

Dad laughed. "No, Destiny. You wouldn't turn pink."

As we drove closer to the flamingo area, I could see several beautiful bright pink flamingos. Many of the birds stood wading in the water, while others rested in muddy, shaded areas. We laid their food on the ground and watched as they turned their heads upside down.

"What are they doing?" I asked, laughing.

"Flamingos are very interesting to watch when eating. First of all, they hold their breath while turning their heads upside down. Their bill sucks in water and food, and then mud and water are expelled from the back of their bills."

"That's incredible!" I voiced. "I don't think I could eat upside down," I said, trying to turn my head like the flamingos.

Dad tried it too, and we both started laughing.

There were so many flamingos to take pictures of that I hope I got some good ones. When we finished caring for these birds, we headed back toward the truck. As I was climbing, I noticed a frog resting on a lily pad. It was so cute! Click! Click!

"Next stop, toucans, cockatoos, and macaws," Dad said.

Once we arrived at the next site, we placed some containers of seeds, fruits, and nuts into each of their large enclosures. I was so excited seeing these beautiful birds. The multicolored feathers on the macaw's body were stunning. The toucans, with their black feathers, gorgeous blue eyes, and long colorful bills, were captivating, and the cockatoos were breathtaking with their white feathers and bright orange perch and wings. They were a sight to see. It was so much fun watching all of these birds flying about in their screened-in areas. I must have taken thirty pictures.

"I love these birds!" I said to my dad. "What can you tell me about the macaws?" I asked.

"Macaws are in the parrot family. They are very intelligent, social birds that typically gather in flocks of ten to thirty birds. They vocalize to communicate within the flock, to mark their territory, and to identify each other. Some can even mimic a human's voice."

"Do any of the macaws talk?" I asked.

"Yes, Harmony does. He says hello to everyone that comes to see him."

"Well then, let's go say hi! I always heard that birds could talk, but I've never heard one," I said.

We walked over to see Harmony, and as soon as he finished playing with some bells, he cocked his head, looked at me, and said, "Hello!"

"Hello, pretty bird," I voiced with a smile.

"Hello! Hello!" he repeated.

"I think he likes you," Dad said.

"Well, I like you too, Harmony," I said.

As we left Harmony and the many other beautiful macaws, we headed to the toucans.

"Dad, why are the toucan's bills so big?"

"The toucan's bill is a honeycomb of bone and is used to catch their food, for attracting a mate, and to keep cool in warm climates. It can also be used as a weapon to scare off predators."

"I don't think that I would want to be bitten by a toucan's bill. It would hurt," I said.

"Yes, it would. We are very careful with all the animals so that we don't get injured," Dad said.

"I do love the color of their bill, though, and their pretty blue eyes." Click! Click! Click!

"Me too," Dad said.

"How long is their bill?" I asked.

"The average bill is eight inches long," Dad said.

"One more question, Dad. Why are there so many holes in the trees?" I asked.

"Toucans like to sleep in the holes of the trees and roll up into a ball to appear small," Dad explained.

"Cool!"

We waved goodbye to the toucans and headed out.

"Hey, Destiny, how would you like to meet Peaches, the cockatoo?" Dad asked.

"Oh, yes! I would like that very much!" I answered.

"Peaches," Dad said, "is a creamy, peach-colored cockatoo with an orange crest and wings. Would you like to hold her?" Dad asked.

"Yes!"

Peaches is a very sweet cockatoo and likes to talk. My dad took her off the perch, and I stroked her soft feathers. He then placed her gently on my arm. She stood still for a moment and then quickly walked up my shoulders and then down to my chest. She looked around and then rested her head on my shoulders.

"Awww. You're right, Dad, she is very sweet."

Suddenly, she picked up her head and loudly voiced, "Peaches! Peaches sweet!"

Dad and I laughed.

I held Peaches for a little while. Then she started to feel heavy, so my dad placed his arm next to my chest and she hopped right up onto his arm.

"Time for Peaches to go back onto her perch," Dad said.

"Thanks for letting me hold her. It was a lot of fun!"

"You're welcome! Destiny, I have a question for you. What bird is the symbol of our country?" Dad asked.

"The American bald eagle," I said.

"Right! You are one smart young lady," he said with a smile. "Let's go and visit them!"

"Yay!"

When we arrived at the eagles' enclosure, my dad explained that the two eagles had been badly injured and that they couldn't be released back into the wild, so now the zoo cares for them.

"Oh my gosh! They're so beautiful!" I said.

"They're fascinating to watch, and you can learn so much from just sitting down and observing them. Actually, it's the best part of my job. It's amazing!" Dad said. "What can you tell me just by watching the eagles, Destiny?"

"I can tell that they are very alert and watching their surroundings with a keen eye."

"You're right, Destiny. Eagles have perfect vision and can see four times better than a human."

"Wow. Look at that nest! It's huge!" I voiced.

"Yes, it is. It's two feet deep and five feet across. It's lined with twigs, grass, moss, and feathers."

"Are there any babies?"

"There are two eggs in the nest. Both the male and female will take turns caring for the eggs. The babies will hatch in about thirty-five days," Dad said.

"This is very exciting!" I said. "I want to come back and see the babies."

"Sounds good to me," Dad said with a smile.

Before leaving, we slid some fish into their enclosure and then climbed back into the truck.

"Destiny, how about we take a little break and head over to the Lion's Den to grab a snack?" Dad suggested.

"Sounds good to me," I said as I wiped the sweat from the heat of the sun off my brow.

When we arrived at the Lion's Den, I looked over the menu on the wall and asked the young woman behind the counter for a Fruity Giraffe. It had pineapple, strawberries, cantaloupe, and bananas on a long stick. My dad ordered a Chunky Monkey, which was a large frozen banana covered in chocolate and nuts.

"Are you enjoying yourself this morning, Destiny?" Dad asked.

"Oh, yes. I'm having a great time with you, Daddy!" I said.

"I love having you with me today, sunshine," he said, giving me a hug.

"Thanks, Daddy! I love being with you too!" We sat down on a bench under a shaded purple jacaranda tree. It was still early in the day, but a lot of work had been done. So resting felt good.

"Okay, Dad, I'm all rested, and my tummy is happy. Let's go!" I said, being a little antsy.

"Let's go see the elephants!" Dad said.

As we made our way to the elephants, Dad told me that elephants are a very intelligent species. They are the largest land mammal in the world, and they have the largest brain in the animal kingdom. They can weigh over eleven thousand pounds. Elephants also have incredible memories, can cry and laugh, and are sensitive.

"Wow, that's amazing! Oh, look, a baby elephant!" I said as I looked out the window.

"Her name is Sweetness, and she's a very sweet calf."

As we approached the elephant area, many of the animals were in the mud, and some were throwing dirt on themselves.

"What are the elephants doing?" I asked.

"Their skin is tough with ridged ceases and very thick, while some areas are soft and supple. Elephants lack sweat glands, so mud baths cool them down. Elephants throw dirt on themselves as a way to protect their skin from the hot sun."

When we arrived, we headed towards the first enclosure. My dad asked me to remain in the safe zone and observe them until he came back with Sweetness. One by one, the elephants were bathed by employees. I could tell the elephants enjoyed their baths, as some swung their long trunks and a few held on to a water hose. Once the zookeepers began to bathe the calf's mother, my dad brought Sweetness into the safe zone.

I asked, "How much did she weigh at birth?"

"At birth, she weighed two hundred pounds and was two and a half feet tall. Since her birth, she has gained thirty pounds a week."

"Oh, my goodness!"

"Okay, Sweetness, it's your turn!" Dad said.

My dad filled up a bucket with soapy water and handed me a brush. Sweetness didn't stop moving the whole time, so it was a challenge to wash her, but it was fun. Luckily, we threw on raincoats, or we'd have been soaked. We hosed her off, and then Dad led her back to her mother.

"That was fun, and you are right, Dad. Sweetness is a very sweet girl." Once the baths were finished, several bales of hay were placed into the elephants' bins and fresh water was placed into their pool. Dad told me that adult elephants can eat up to 660 pounds of food in a single day and that they drink about thirty gallons of water daily.

"Wow, that's incredible. I think I would blow up if I drank that much water!" I said, laughing.

"Now that was a job. How about we take a break and head over to the craft center?" Dad asked.

"Okay." We walked into the Wildlife Craft Center, where my dad introduced me to Kathy.

"Hello, Destiny! Welcome to the craft center!" Kathy said.

"Hello!" I said.

My dad told me that Kathy is a lovely, kind woman and that she has a new granddaughter named Holly.

"Congratulations!" I said.

"Thank you, my dear!" she said as she happily pulled out a photo of Holly.

"Awww. She's so cute! I love babies!" I said.

"Me too!" Kathy said. "I'm glad you're here! How would you like to make an animal mask?"

"What type of mask?" I asked.

"I'll show you. Come follow me to the craft table," she said.

We walked over to where there were several masks.

"Hmm," I said. "A lion, no. A monkey, no. A tiger, no."

"How about a koala?" Kathy asked. "Your dad told me how much you love koalas."

"Yes, I do!"

"Okay, then. A koala mask it is!" Kathy smiled.

Kathy handed me the crayons, and I colored my mask. She then handed me some string to attach to the sides of the mask.

"Nice job!" Dad said as he tied the mask on.

"Donny," Kathy said, speaking to my dad, "have you told Destiny about the surprise at the zoo?"

"Not yet, but I will soon," he chuckled.

I thanked Kathy for the mask as my dad and I left the craft center.

"You're welcome, Destiny!" Kathy said, smiling as she waved goodbye. "Have a wonderful day!"

"You too," I voiced. "What surprise is Kathy talking about?"

"You'll just have to wait, my dear," Dad said teasingly.

"This mask is hot to wear," I said as I took it off.

We climbed back up into my dad's truck, drove down a dirt road, and parked under a shady tree.

"Let's carry some food with us and walk down the Australian path," Dad said. "How would you like to see some amazing Australian animals?" he asked.

"Let's go!" I said excitedly.

"First, I want to show you an incredibly large bird," Dad told me.

"What is it?"

"You'll see," Dad replied.

"Whoa! That is the biggest bird I have ever seen! What is it?" I asked.

"It's called a double-wattled cassowary. It is one of the largest flightless birds, weighing one hundred twenty-eight pounds, and they are extremely dangerous.

It has a helmet of tough skin on its head called a casque, which acts as a shovel to assist the cassowary in searching for food through the dense vegetation of the tropical rainforest. Its coarse black feathers protect the bird from any undergrowth vegetation," Dad said.

"I love the blue face and red on its neck," I told my dad. It's very pretty. I took several pictures of this amazing bird and said, "Wait till Mom sees this!"

Dad carried the cassowary's tray of food, slid it through a door, and then closed it. Just when the food was placed, the cassowary came out from the bushes.

"They're beautiful birds, with powerful legs and three toes, and dagger-like claws on their inner toes that are up to four inches long. The cassowary's legs enable it to jump up to five feet and run up to thirty miles per hour," Dad said.

"Wow! Can you imagine if you ran into one of these birds in the rainforest? Yikes! Let's move on, Dad," I voiced.

We continued down the path and saw many remarkable Australian animals. We left food and water for many of the animals, but my favorite was the kangaroos.

"Awww, look, a baby joey in his mama's pouch," I said.

"She sure is cute. Her name is Hoppy," Dad said. "Destiny, did you know that kangaroos are marsupials?" Dad asked.

"Yes, I did, just like koalas," I replied. "I also know that marsupials have pouches to hold their young and care for them," I said.

My dad also told me that kangaroos are the only large animal that can move forward by hopping on their strong legs and large feet, yet they cannot hop backwards. Their large and strong tail can be used for balance or as a fifth limb when using their front and back legs.

We fed the kangaroos, got them some fresh water, and cleaned up their enclosure. It was so fun to watch them hop around.

"Ready to move on?" Dad asked.

"Let's hop along to the next animal!" I said.

"You're so cute!" Dad said with a smile. "Now, are you ready for your big surprise?" Dad asked.

"Yes!" I said, jumping up and down.

"I want you to take my hand and close your eyes, and don't open them until I say," Dad voiced.

We walked a few steps, and he turned me around.

"Keep them closed, Destiny," he said again. "Now, on the count of three, open your eyes," Dad said. "One. Two. Three!"

I opened my eyes to see the most incredible thing. It was a family of koalas. I was so excited! I ran up to my dad and gave him a big hug. "When did they come? Where? How?"

"Slow down, Destiny! I'll tell you. The koalas came from Australia about a month ago, but they were quarantined and I couldn't show you until they were cleared by the veterinarians. While in quarantine, we prepared their enclosure." My dad pointed to each koala as he called out their names, Hogan, Ash, Desiree, Poppy, and baby Lily.

"Koalas! I'm so excited." Click! Click! Click! went my camera.

"Would you like to hold one?" Dad asked.

"Oh, my goodness. Really!"

"Oh, yes!" my dad said with a big smile.

My dad gently took a koala off a tree branch and carefully placed him in my arms. His name is Hogan, and he's a gray and white koala. He's a heavy boy, and a little stinky, but soft and cute as could be. A tear ran down my cheek as I held him. This had always been a dream of mine, to hold my favorite animal, and now it had come true. I was so happy. It was an incredible experience. After some time, Dad placed Hogan in the tree, and then I hugged him, saying, "Thank you! Thank you! I will never forget this day."

"So, tell me, Destiny. What do you know about koalas?"

"I know that koalas are native to Australia, they are not bears, and they spend most of their time in a tree, sleeping eighteen to twenty hours a day. They have sharp claws to climb trees, their fingerprints are similar to humans', their babies are called joeys, and they eat eucalyptus leaves. Oh, yes, and they don't typically drink water. They get their moisture from the leaves."

"Very good! I'm impressed, young lady."

"I know my koalas," I chuckled. "I even know what causes them to sleep so much."

"Tell me," Dad asked.

"It's the eucalyptus leaves."

"You really do know your koalas," Dad said.

"Yes, I do!" I said with a smile.

Before leaving the koalas, we placed several eucalyptus branches in the trees for them to enjoy. I could have stayed with the koalas all day.

"Can I come and visit the koalas often now that you have them at the zoo?" I asked.

"I expected this. Of course! I don't think I could keep you away," he chuckled. "Destiny, now that all my animal friends are fed, we can drive the truck back to the employee parking area and enjoy the rest of the day touring the zoo," Dad said.

"Sounds great!"

"Let's start with the camels."

"Cool!" I said.

"Camels are truly spectacular to watch," my dad told me.

"Dad, do camels really have water in their humps?"

"No, camels do not store water in their humps. It's actually a reservoir of fatty tissue that helps the camel survive under the intense heat of the sun. Camels can, however, drink up to twenty-six gallons of water at a time."

"Wow!"

"Did you know that camels can swim?" Dad said.

"Really!" I voiced, surprised. "Now that is pretty cool. I'd like to see that," I said, laughing.

"Let's walk closer to the camels' enclosure," Dad said. My dad picked me up closer to the camel so I could see him better.

"He's very handsome. What's his name?" I asked.

"Bruno," Dad said.

"Well, Bruno, you're a big boy, and you have a big head and large, pretty eyes."

"He sure does," Dad said.

Just as my dad placed me back on the ground, a zookeeper came and led Bruno to another area.

"Where's he going with Bruno?" I asked.

"That gentleman cares for the camels and works with them. He loves his camels. The gentleman's name is Sebastian. He is getting the camels ready for the children to ride," Dad said as we watched him prepare the camels for the rides.

"Would you like to ride Bruno? They are about to start the camel rides," Dad asked.

"Sure!"

I was the first one in line for the ride. I stepped up onto the platform as my dad introduced me to Sebastian. Sebastian welcomed me as he helped me get up onto the brown, one-humped camel. The camel had a soft blanket on its back and a small carriage-like seat with soft lining to hold on to. I held on tightly to the carriage bars as Sebastian walked alongside the camel. It was a bumpy ride and really high up, but fun.

As we walked around in a circle, Sebastian began to tell me about Bruno. He said that Bruno is a pretty brown camel with thick fur, big eyes, long legs, and large, flat feet. Camels have two sets of eyelashes to keep the sand out of their eyes

and flat feet to walk in the desert. Bruno is over seven feet tall and weighs 1,800 pounds. He can drink several gallons of water in minutes. I patted Bruno's soft fur and waved to my dad as I finished the ride. I thanked Sebastian as he helped me down and led me to my dad.

"That was so much fun, and I learned a lot about Bruno," I voiced. "I'm hungry. Can we go back to the Lion's Den to get something to eat?"

"Sure, I'm hungry too!" he replied. "Let's go!" So we headed to lunch at the Lion's Den. We looked over the menu and placed our order. I ordered a Lion's Roar Burger with some Grassy Fries, and a Macaw's Fruity Shake, which was a cheeseburger, french fries, and a fruity shake. My dad ordered a Cock-Doodle-Do Triple Decker Sandwich with Skunk Rings, and a Zebra's Stripe Shake. I liked the sound of a chicken sandwich, onions rings, and a chocolate shake, but I changed my mind. After we picked up our meals, we walked over to a wooden picnic table under another beautiful jacaranda tree and sat down.

"This is a great place to sit. I can see the lions. Roarrr."

"That was pretty fierce, Destiny," Dad said. "You must be hungry. Let's eat before the beast comes out again," Dad laughed.

"My food is yummy!" I voiced.

"Mine is pretty good too," he said.

As we were eating, I said, "I love watching lions. The males are so big with their large manes. I wish I could hug one, but I know that's impossible."

"You are very wise for your young age," Dad said.

Suddenly, oh my goodness! "Dad, look!" I said as I jumped up. The lioness was lying down next to the lion, and when she stood up, the lion got upset and

roared loudly, showing his large teeth, as did she. The lion then got up and followed her, roaring again as she settled back down next to him. Boy, that was exciting and a little scary.

"Everything is all right, Destiny," Dad said as he gently touched my hand. "Come sit down." Dad asked, "Did you know that a lion's fierce roar can be heard up to five miles away?"

"I believe it!" I said.

"Lions are aggressive, territorial, and social with their group or pride. Lions live in prides of mainly females. They have vision five times greater than we do, and after the tiger, lions are the biggest wild cats in the world."

"Why do they have such large manes?" I asked.

"It's to protect them while fighting other lions."

Now that the lions had settled down, we finished eating our meal and then continued our walk around the zoo.

"Next stop, tigers!" Dad said.

"I love tigers!" I voiced.

"They're magnificent!" Dad said.

We walked up to the large, fenced enclosure and saw two gorgeous, striped tigers resting under a shaded tree. One tiger with blue eyes had a distinctive white coat with black stripes, while the other had brown eyes and was golden in color with black stripes. "They're so beautiful!" I said in awe. Click! Click! Click! "They sure are big cats!"

"Yes, they are, and very powerful and extremely territorial. They are

great swimmers and can leap forward up to thirty-three feet," Dad said.

"Very impressive," I said.

"And like the giraffe and zebra, each tiger has its own distinctive pattern of stripes."

"Cool!" I voiced.

I watched as the white tiger came up to the tall fence and began pacing back and forth. It was fantastic to be that close to such an incredible animal. Then I went over to another viewing area to see the golden tiger. It was just lying up on the grassy area, looking down at us. He was a beautiful tiger.

As the afternoon came upon us, we visited some interesting animals, a few rhinoceros and a baby, a red panda, panda bears, polar bears, and peacocks. Click! Click! Click! I was genuinely overjoyed with every moment of the day. I took many pictures of these beautiful animals, and my dad told me that when I came back to the zoo another day, he would teach me more about these wonderful animals.

"Destiny, I want you to see a few more animals, and then we'll think about heading home," Dad said.

"Great, let's go!"

"Gorillas are next," Dad said. "I want to check on the male gorilla. He was sick for a few days and needs some tender, loving care. He's feeling better today and is outside with his family."

Gorillas are so amazing to watch. The male gorilla was huge, and his eyes were so intense. I wondered what he was thinking. My dad told me that gorillas are a lot like humans and are very intelligent.

After seeing the family of gorillas interact, I believed they were pretty smart. I saw how gentle a mother gorilla was with her young baby as she cradled it in her arms. It was beautiful and warmed my heart.

Suddenly, as we were standing near the enclosure watching the gorillas, we heard some loud screaming from behind us.

"What animal is making all that noise?" I asked.

Dad laughed and said, "Those are gibbons." He told me that gibbons are very vocal and territorial.

"I guess so!" I laughed.

"Let's sit down and rest here, Destiny," Dad said. By now, my steps were getting slower and my eyes were getting heavy. It had been a long day. While resting, we watched these energetic, acrobatic primates swing from tree to tree, and rope to rope. I loved looking at their sweet, little faces. Their faces are hairless and black, and they have bright, dark eyes and little

noses surrounded by a ring of white hair. The rest of their body is covered in gorgeous, thick golden hair. Just as I closed my eyes for a second, the loud screaming sounds started again, causing me to jump. My dad looked down at me and asked, "Are you getting tired, Destiny?"

"Yes."

"What do you say we head home?"

"Sounds good." We walked back to my dad's truck and climbed in. The horizon was beginning to turn into brilliant shades of pinks and purples as the sun set. It was beautiful and a nice way to end our day.

I had a wonderful day with my dad at the zoo, and I learned so much about the animals. When we arrived home, we enjoyed our supper as we talked about our day.

"It was a lovely day," I told my mom.

"I can see how tired you are," Mom said.

"I sure am," I replied.

After supper, I played with my stuffed animals and then got ready for bed.

Once in bed, I was tucked in, and my parents wished me sweet dreams.

The next morning when I awoke, I asked my mom to print out the zoo pictures from the camera and help me make a scrapbook. It was really fun to make. It was a truly memorable day, one that I won't forget anytime soon, the day I went to the zoo.

Printed in the United States
By Bookmasters